BENJIE'S HAT

Books by
MABEL LEIGH HUNT

———

Lucinda: A Little Girl of 1860
The Boy Who Had No Birthday
Little Girl With Seven Names
Susan, Beware!

BENJIE'S HAT

By

MABEL LEIGH HUNT

Illustrated by GRACE PAULL

J. B. LIPPINCOTT COMPANY
PHILADELPHIA   NEW YORK

To
BOBBY WRIGHT,
WHO MIGHT HAVE BEEN ANOTHER BENJIE,
HAD HE LIVED EIGHTY YEARS AGO

AND

To
PEARL IDOL,
WHO ONCE TOLD ME A STORY OF
A BENJIE WHO DID LIVE EIGHTY YEARS AGO

BENJIE'S HAT

CHAPTER I

Sometimes it takes a boy years and years of steady growing to become big enough and tall enough to match the name that his parents gave him.

That is how it was with Benjie. For although he had been busily growing for eight years, the name of Benjamin Bartholomew Barnett was still much too large for him. So he was called Benjie, except in very serious moments.

Benjie was a little Quaker boy, and his home was in North Carolina, where a great many other Quakers lived, though they did not call themselves Quakers, but *Friends*. Which is a very warm and beautiful word, when you stop to think about it.

In all his eight years, Benjie had never been anywhere except over into the next county to visit his grandmother, Judith Cox. But in spite of never having traveled, he was a very happy boy. Only— sometimes he lost his temper and sulked a bit because his two older brothers, Milo and Matthew, seemed to think that he was still just a baby, and left him to play with his sisters, Hannah, who was a fat little girl with fat flaxen braids, and Narcissa Clementina, who was a fatter little girl, with fatter and more flaxen braids. And although Benjie loved

Hannah and Narcissa Clementina, he himself had left off wearing skirts years ago. He was also of the opinion that this world is a man's world, and that he was well on the way toward being a man himself.

Someone else thought so, too, and a proud day was to come for Benjie.

One day in September a neighbor of Grandmother's came riding to Randolph County, where Benjie lived. His name was Peter Kersey, and he was an Elder of the Deep River Monthly Meeting, over in Guilford County, where Grandmother lived. He had come on business of his own, but he stopped at Benjie's house, and had dinner there, and he left a letter from Grandmother. Although this letter was addressed to the whole family, Benjie heard and remembered only one amazing paragraph.

"I want Benjie to come and spend the winter with me," wrote Grandmother. "The schoolhouse is only a mile through the woods, so that it will be right smart easier for him here than at home. Tell him that I am very lonely since his grandfather died,

[3]

and that I need a manbody to look after me and keep me company."

"A manbody!"

Benjie looked at Milo and Matthew. And then he threw out his chest, and stiffened his neck and thrust his hands in his pockets. For Milo and Matthew were staring at him in quite a surprised manner, as if to say, "Look here! Who's *this* Grandmother is calling a 'manbody?' Surely not little Benjie!"

And Milo, who was thirteen, said, "*I* could go, Mother."

And Matthew, who was eleven, said, "Maybe she meant *me*, Mother."

But Mother said, "No, it's Benjie Grandmother wants, and it's Benjie who shall go."

So perhaps it is not surprising that Benjie felt there was no one in all of North Carolina quite as important as Benjamin Bartholomew Barnett. Unless it might be the Governor. But—"a manbody!" Well, wasn't he eight years old? *Of course* he could look after Grandmother!

And, too, he remembered the molasses cookies in the big stone jar in Grandmother's kitchen— always plenty of them. And when he went to bed that night, he lay awake as long as five minutes thinking of all the pleasant and interesting things he would do and see again at Grandmother's house. He wondered if his friend Eliphalet would be glad to see him, and if Jerushy, the speckled hen, who was already nearly thirteen years old, was still alive. He wondered if Grandmother had grown any pea-nuts this year, and as he fell asleep, it seemed to him that he could actually taste the rich, waxy molasses cookies from Grandmother's cooky jar.

So the very next morning, quite early, Benjie dressed himself for the journey to Guilford County. He put on the tow shirt and breeches that Mother had woven from the coarse part of the flax and then tailored into a neat suit. He put on the shoes and stockings that in the summer time he wore only to Meeting. And after breakfast he put on the round straw hat that had first been Milo's, and then Matthew's, and now had descended to Benjie.

It had been a store hat, and Milo had been extremely proud of it. Matthew had been a little less proud of it, and Benjie was not proud of it at all. He wore it without thinking much about it, though sometimes it did occur to him that it would would be nice to have a hat that had never belonged to any one else. But you must endure hand-me-downs, if you happen to be the third boy in the family.

During the hat's descent from brother to brother, its edges had become torn and frayed, but Mother had bound them very neatly all around with a strip of gray flannel. There was a torn place in the crown, too, which she had darned with knitting yarn into a kind of a design, just as if it were intended to be that way. This morning, preparing to go to Grandmother's, Benjie was too excited to give the hat a thought.

The time came to depart. Benjie's father slung

Peter Kersey's saddle-bags over the horse's saddle, for Peter had kindly consented to have Benjie's few belongings packed into one of the bags. Then Benjie was hoisted up. Benjie's mother thought that her son looked very small behind Peter's broad back. Her lips trembled as she waved farewell, and Benjie, much to his surprise, suddenly felt as if he might be going to cry if Peter didn't hurry off at once. Which of course would have been very strange behavior for "a manbody."

Fat little Hannah was crying, and wiping her wet cheeks on a fold of Mother's skirt. But then she was only a girl. Fat Narcissa Clementina was crying, too, and wiping her wet cheeks on the other side of Mother's skirt, but she was a mere baby, and was crying just because Hannah was crying. Which is a very foolish reason for crying at all.

Milo and Matthew were staring at Benjie as if at last they considered him a SOMEBODY, as well as "a manbody," and the sight of his brothers' envy was so cheering to Benjie that he grinned joyfully

back at everyone, and gave the horse a little dig with his heel.

So Peter Kersey and Benjamin Bartholomew Barnett rode away to Guilford County, to Grandmother's house.

[8]

Chapter II

Benjie liked living at Grandmother's from the moment of his arrival. In the first place he loved his Grandmother. In the second place, in Grandmother's house he was the only boy. He was important, and not just Milo and Matthew's little brother. Grandmother treated him as if she really considered him "a manbody," or at least well on the way.

In the third place, out of the iron pots slung over the hearth fire, and from the big outdoor oven on baking days, there came the most savory and delicious foods, for Grandmother was as famous for her cooking as she was for her thrifty ways. The molasses cookies were even bigger and browner and better than Benjie remembered.

Grandmother lived in a comfortable old house

built of great, hand-hewn timbers. The oaken floors were always well scrubbed, the hand-woven coverlets and rugs always bright, the pewter always gleaming, and Grandmother herself, in kerchief and cap, as neat as a plump little sparrow.

Though Grandmother lived in great comfort on her fertile farm, she was very careful and thrifty. People respected her for it, too, but sometimes they would smile, and say, "as thrifty as Friend Judith Cox." Grandmother had worn her best bonnet to Meeting every First Day for twelve years, but it was just as stiff and neat as it was the day she had carried it home from the bonnet-maker's so long ago. Grandmother expected it to last her the remainder of her days. Her best silk dress and her second-best delaine were folded away in old linen when she wasn't wearing one or the other of them. Her shawls had not a hole in them. Her white kerchiefs lasted an amazingly long time. In the house there were chests and boxes and barrels and old trunks full of things that Grandmother would never dream of casting aside. She considered it a grievous sin to throw even a pin away, and in her sewing-box there was a certain needle for which she had a great attachment. She showed it to Benjie. "I have been using this same needle for eight years! I made one of thy baby dresses with it." And she added:

"Thee must always be careful of what thee has, Benjie. 'Wilful waste, woeful want.' If thee will think upon that, thee will understand what it means. Waste is an abomination in the sight of the Lord."

And although Benjie knew what she meant, it is to be feared that he thought more about what a funny word "abomination" was, and that it might be a good one to try on Eliphalet.

For on Seventh Days, when there was no school, Benjie often played with Eliphalet.

Eliphalet was nine years old. He was the son of Hamish and Dilcey, the free negroes who lived in a cabin on Grandmother's farm. Together the boys explored the banks of the slow, amber-colored river, or roamed through the woods, gathering the sweet wild muscadines, and as they ripened, nuts and per-simmons. Benjie and Eliphalet were great friends.

Hamish was very good at picking the banjo, and on mild September evenings, Grandmother and Benjie could hear the rippling *twang*, *twang* coming up faintly through the corn-field, as Hamish played

his favorite tunes. Once in a while Grandmother would allow Benjie to go to the cabin when Hamish was playing. He would sit on the porch, a little fair-haired boy surrounded by the kindly, shining black faces of Hamish and Dilcey and Eliphalet, and sometimes two cronies of Hamish, named Alec and Phin, who were slaves on a plantation down the road toward Jamestown. Benjie always knew when Alec and Phin were bound for Hamish's cabin, because they had to come to Grandmother's house first, to show their passes. These were pieces of paper, something like tickets. They had been made out by the master of the plantation, and they allowed Alec and Phin to visit with Hamish for two hours. Alec and Phin had to be very careful never to stay longer than the two hours. If they did, the patrol, or "patteroll," as he was commonly called, would come after them.

Alec and Phin were almost as good at picking the banjo as Hamish. When the three of them played together, it seemed to Benjie as if the gay little notes spilled out of the banjos and danced all over the floor of the porch and all around the cabin, tripping gaily in and out among the big ripening leaves of the tobacco-patch, out among the bare patches of corn, making the dark shadows of the pines out yonder as comfortable and friendly as Hamish and Alec and Phin themselves. And sometimes the little notes would be sad ones that seemed to strike at Benjie's heart and make him wish he had something nice to give to Alec and Phin.

But life was not all play at Grandmother's house. Benjie had his chores, too, throwing down hay for the horses, turning the windlass that drew the water from the covered well, driving the cows to and from the pasture, feeding the pigs and the chickens. He always threw the choicest morsels to Jerushy, the speckled hen that was almost thirteen years old, for he thought she deserved excellent treatment, and indeed she had the respect of everyone on the farm. The people roundabout knew of her, too, and spoke of her as "Judith Cox's ancient

hen." She hadn't laid an egg for years, and Grandmother said, "Jerushy doesn't earn her board and
keep, but I declare I never can bear to kill the vali-
ant old creature."

In the evenings, while Grandmother knitted busily, she and Benjie would play riddles and guessing games, and Grandmother would tell stories. Benjie would read his lessons to Grandmother, too. She always seemed to enjoy them much better than he did. Afterward Grandmother would read a chapter from the big Bible. Then early to bed, and the long, long night of sleep.

So Benjie was a happy boy, and felt sure that his winter with Grandmother was going to be a great success.

"Am I looking after thee and keeping thee company, like thee said in thy letter, Grandmother?" asked Benjie.

"Thee is very satisfactory," answered Grandmother. "Thee is a regular little manbody."

CHAPTER III

Every First Day, which was Sunday, Hamish
hitched the horse to the carriage. Grandmother put
on her best bonnet and one of her good dresses and
her softest, finest kerchief. Benjie cleaned his shoes
and scrubbed his cheeks and put on his tow suit and
the straw hat bound round with gray flannel. He
and Grandmother climbed into the carriage.
Grandmother took up the reins, clucked to the
horse, and off they went to Meeting.

When they arrived at the meeting-house,
Grandmother patted Benjie's shoulder, and said,
"Now thee be a good boy, Grandson," which was
rather unnecessary, as Benjie behaved himself very
well indeed. He may have squirmed a little when
his feet went to sleep, or when the day was warm
and his tow breeches scratched him, but that was all.

Then he and Grandmother parted, for Grandmother must sit on the women's side of the meeting-house with the women and girls, and Benjie must sit with the men on the men's side. He felt very grown-up sitting there without his father and Milo and Matthew, as at home, and for several First Days this was enough to keep Benjie completely satisfied throughout the long silent meeting. For when Benjie was a little boy, the Friends had no music at their religious services, and only rarely did they have preaching. Children must "wait in stillness upon the Lord," as their elders did, and receive comfort and strength through silent meditation and prayer.

On a certain October morning Benjie and Grandmother went to meeting. There never was a more perfect day. The long needles of the pines glittered in the golden sunlight. The red and golden leaves fluttered lazily down from the trees that were all red and golden. Through the open windows of the meeting-house Benjie could hear the horses moving lazily and stamping at their hitching-racks. From afar came the whistle of quail. For the first time Benjie felt fidgety. The coarse stuff of his clothing made him itch, and although no one paid him any attention, he knew that he must not scratch. The world outside seemed to be saying, "Come out, Benjie. Come out and play in the golden morning." Benjie kept hearing this soft and golden voice, and as there seemed to be no probability of the meeting ever coming to an end, and as the prickles on his legs seemed to be getting worse, he arose at last from his place, very softly. He squeezed past several large knees, whose owners looked at him gravely from under their broad hats. But Benjie knew that they scarcely saw him, for their thoughts were far removed from worldly things. He tiptoed down the aisle of the men's side and out into the meeting-house grounds.

The stillness outside was almost as deep as it had been in the meeting-house, a charmed and golden stillness, and Benjie, now that he had come, scarcely knew what to do with himself. It was very queer, but he didn't itch a bit any more. He looked about, and felt lonely. The world seemed an empty golden shell, with no one in it but the horses and a stranger named Benjamin Bartholomew Barnett. Oh, dear, whatever had made him come? How shocked and sorry Grandmother would be if she knew that he had run away from Meeting! A little lump came into Benjie's throat when he thought of Grandmother, whom he loved so much, and who loved him. Forlornly he wandered to the fence and began to stroke the noses of the horses, since there was no joy for him in the lovely day, after all. He gathered handfuls of grass for them. They nosed him eagerly.

And then a most surprising thing happened. For all of a sudden Benjie heard a loud crunching noise. His head was jerked violently sidewise. A damp breath blew through his hair, and he looked up to see an old white horse at his shoulder. And he had Benjie's hat in his mouth. He was chewing with all his might and main. He was chewing up

Benjie's hat!

"Ow!" cried Benjie. "Gimme my hat!" He reached up as far as he could and began tugging at the object that was no longer a hat, but a crushed and mangled fragment. A long strip of gray flannel hung from the horse's mouth. Bits of straw fell to the ground. The hat was gone, all but one little piece in Benjie's hand—the hat that had been a fine store hat, the hat that had once been Milo's pride, that had been worn less proudly by Matthew, and was, until a moment ago, Benjie's only hat.

Oh, the mean old horse! The meanest old horse in the world! What could Benjie do? He couldn't slip back into Meeting and sit with uncovered head. That was unthinkable, for the Friends wore their hats throughout the Meeting. What would Grandmother say when she found that Benjie had not only "played hooky" from Meeting, but had lost his hat as well. "Wilful waste, woeful want," that's what Grandmother would say. Oh, she would think him a very bad boy! Well, he was, although he hadn't really meant to be. Losing his hat was a punishment for stealing away from Meeting. At last Benjie climbed up into Grandmother's carriage, with the one remnant of his hat in his hand, and made himself as small as possible.

Presently the people began coming slowly out of the meeting-house, looking refreshed and calm and cheerful. They shook hands with each other in the autumn sunshine. There was a pleasant hum of talk.

Benjie screwed himself into a tighter knot on the carriage seat, but kept a weather eye open for Grandmother. Yes, there she was! Beloved Grandmother, folded so neatly into her shawl, her face placid and rosy in its neat frame of bonnet. There! She was looking for him! Oh, dear! Benjie turned his head away sadly. He couldn't bear to see Grandmother looking for the *good* boy that should have come out of the meeting-house with all the good people when Meeting broke.

And then he heard the soft rustle of Grandmother's skirts. He felt her near him.

"Why, Benjie-boy!" she cried. "Is thee ill? Did thee have to leave the Meeting?"

"No, Grandmother," answered Benjie. He turned and looked at her, full of misery. "I didn't have to leave. Just see what happened, Grandmother." He held out the piece of straw. "An old horse chewed up my hat!"

"Thy hat! Benjie! Does thee mean to say that a horse reached into the meeting-house and took the very hat off thy head? Never did I hear the like!" And as Grandmother climbed into the carriage she looked about indignantly as if to say, "Where is that rude creature that ate the hat off the grandson of Judith Cox?"

"Oh, no, Grandmother!" Benjie could not help smiling a little at the impossible picture that Grandmother had imagined. Nothing short of a giraffe could have reached into the meeting-house.

"No, Grandmother," he went on. "I did leave Meeting. It's a nice day, and my pants scratched me, and my feet were going to sleep, and before I thought what I was doing, I was walking out of Meeting."

"Benjamin Bartholomew Barnett!" exclaimed Grandmother. "Thee left Meeting just because thee was fidgety?"

"But I didn't have a bit good time, Grandmother!" cried Benjie hastily. "I wished and wished
I hadn't come. And then the old horse grabbed my
hat. If he'd just waited a minute I'd have given him
some nice grass. I was taking turns feeding them all
grass. But he couldn't wait—the old greedy!"

"A just punishment for thee, Benjie," declared
Grandmother. "Now thee has no hat. And thee
sinned besides." Grandmother shook her head sor-
rowfully.

"Maybe next year the hat would've been too
small for me, Grandmother," suggested Benjie.

"That does not alter the situation, Grandson.
Some other boy could have worn it."

The remainder of the ride home was very quiet.
Dinner was very quiet. The afternoon bade fair to
be very quiet and very long. So that the sound of
the music from Hamish's banjo twanging across the
October fields was welcome to Benjie, even though
it was so surprising. He looked at Grandmother

quickly. Her mouth was set in a straight line.

"Someone else sinneth," she said. "Go down, Benjamin, and ask Hamish what he means by playing the banjo on my farm on First Day. And come back the moment thy errand is done."

Benjie went along the edge of the corn-field, going to meet the gay little banjo notes that seemed to be running, in spite of First Day, to meet him. And there was Hamish, seated in his doorway, his

head bent over his beloved banjo, his fingers strumming happily. And there was Eliphalet, doing a buck-an'-wing in the red-colored dust in front of the cabin.

"Hamish!" cried Benjie sternly. "Grandmother says thee is not to play the banjo on her farm on First Day."

Hamish's mouth fell open. Eliphalet stopped, frozen in his tracks.

"Ah plum fo'got mahes'f," said Hamish, sheepishly. "Reckon hit am de weathah. Reckon hit am a day foh pickin' de banjo. Reckon dis niggah done los' my min' disrememberin' dat Ol' Miss cain' have no music on Fus' Day."

"Grandmother says thee sinneth," announced Benjie. It was rather pleasant to be able to tell Hamish that he, too, was a sinner.

Hamish's face fell. Tenderly he put down his banjo. He looked so sad that Benjie cried, "But I sinned, too, Hamish." And he told his friend all about the morning's sad incident.

At first Hamish looked very sympathetic. But presently his mouth began to spread. The laughter that seemed to have its home in Hamish's toes was coming up, shaking his body, up, up, until it burst from mouth and nose in snorts and chuckles.

"Yoh mean—yoh mean dat ol' white hoss et up dat hat uv yo-alls? Dat ol' white hoss jus' natchally lean hisse'f ovah an' grab dat hat an' chew an' chew twell hit all chewed up?" Hamish flung up his hands in delight. He rocked back and forth, hugging his mirth.

"An' chew an' chew an' chew," echoed Eliphalet. "De hat, de hoss. De hat, de hoss!"

And soon Hamish and Eliphalet and Benjie, too, for he could not help it, were rocking with laughter. And Dilcey came and stood in the doorway. "Dat ol' white hoss don' need no dinnah dis day," she chuckled. "No, 'deedy. He done had a pow'ful good dinnah eatin' off Benjie's hat."

Benjie wished that he could stay in this jolly place. But Grandmother's word was law, and he

trudged dutifully back home. He was relieved to
see that Grandmother seemed much more cheerful.
She and Benjie carried chairs out to the yard and
sat together in the mild autumn sunshine. Presently Jerushy came waddling along, and Grandmother picked her up, and allowed the old hen to
rest upon her aproned lap, for Jerushy and Grandmother were great friends, after all these thirteen
years together.

And while Benjie leaned against Grandmother's chair, and stroked Jerushy's soft old
feathers, Grandmother told him stories. She told
him of his great-grandfather, whose home had been
on Nantucket Island, but who had spent most of
his life at sea, for he had been a whaling master.
"A very good man," said Grandmother. "He held
silent meeting on his ship every First and Fourth
Days, just as if he were in the meeting-house at
home." She told Benjie of his great-uncle, who had
once lain in prison for many weeks, because he re-
fused to bear arms against his fellow-man. She

spoke of Benjie's great-great-grandfather, who had lived in England before sailing to America as a young man, and who had been able to tell his children of the days when George Fox, the great founder of the Society of Friends, used to come to his father's house in that English village where he lived as a boy.

And Grandmother said, "The good people before thee were God-fearing people. *They* had no worldly thoughts at Meeting. None of them would ever have strayed away from Meeting at the slightest excuse, as thee did, Benjamin."

And she looked at Benjie, and Benjie looked at her. It was a long moment, and when it was over, it seemed that Benjie and his Grandmother loved each other even more than ever. And Grandmother reached into her deep pocket, and brought forth a handful of peanuts, and she and Benjie broke them and ate them, which made old Jerushy sit up and jerk her head about, as if to say, "What! Something to eat?" Jerushy made Benjie and Grandmother both smile.

After supper, and six o'clock, when First Day was over, and Benjie was getting ready for bed, he saw Grandmother's eyes begin to twinkle. Her rosy face grew rosier. She held her apron up to her mouth, and she began to shake all over. Grandmother was laughing! It made Benjie laugh to see Grandmother laughing so hard. And when she had calmed down and wiped her eyes, and tucked Benjie into bed, she looked down at him, and she said, "Don't thee be thinking that I considered it funny of thee to run away from Meeting, Benjamin Bartholomew Barnett. It's just the idea of that old horse chewing up thy hat. All of a sudden it struck my funny bone."

And Benjie said, "Grandmother, next First Day I shall go to Meeting, and I shan't *move*, no matter how much my britches scratch me." He suddenly sat up in bed. "But what shall I do? I can't go to Meeting without a hat!"

"That's true, Grandson," answered Grandmother. "And of course it is almost too late in the season to wear thy tow breeches and thy straw hat, anyway. Why didn't thee bring thy winter hat with thee?"

"It was too little for me," said Benjie. "Mother gave it to Cousin Daniel. Mother said that thee would buy me a winter hat over in Friendship."

"Tut, tut!" exclaimed Grandmother. "Does thy mother think that money grows on my peanut vines, or that I dig it up with my yams? But a hat thee must have. That's plain. We'll see what can be done about it. We'll see."

And as Benjie fell asleep, full of Grandmother's loving forgiveness, he thought to himself, "How nice it will be to have a hat all my own, a hat that is bought just for me!"

CHAPTER IV

But the pine woods through which Benjie ran to school still murmured softly of Indian summer, and he did not really need a hat, except for Meeting. So for two days he almost forgot about the hat which had disappeared down the throat of the old white horse. And while he played *Ant'ny-Over* and *Prison Base* with the boys at recess, the thought of a nice new hat lay half-forgotten, too, but warmly treasured in his mind.

On the evening of Third Day, Grandmother said, "To-morrow thee must march with the other children to regular Fourth Day Meeting. Therefore thee must wear thy new hat to school. Thee didn't know I had a surprise for thee, now did thee?"

She opened the door of the fireside cupboard and drew out a hat.

"There, Benjie!" she exclaimed. "While thee was at school, I was busy plying my needle. There was no need to spend good silver, nor good trade, either, for a store hat, when thy grandfather's nap beaver lay unused in its box. See? I cut a mite off the crown, though it was a pity to waste even that bit. I took some pleats in crown and brim, to make it more thy size. Then I sewed them back together again. And there is thy hat!" She held it up proudly.

Benjie stared and stared. "It's a very peculiar-some hat," he murmured, and burst into tears. "The b-b-boys will laugh."

"Tut, tut, Benjie," scolded Grandmother. "Is thee a girl, to be so vain of thy looks? 'Tis a good hat, and 'twill serve the purpose. Thee should feel honored to wear the hat thy grandfather wore for fifteen years."

[34]

Benjie set off for school the next morning, wearing the tall hat. In spite of Grandmother's careful pleatings, it was still much too large for him, and only his ears held it up. In the woods he reached up and felt it carefully. How smooth and furry it was! No doubt Grandfather had once paid a good round sum for it. Perhaps, after all, the boys would not laugh.

But when Benjie entered the school yard, up went shouts of derision, and soon the whole world, as it seemed to Benjie, was echoing with the chorus:

"Look at Benjie's ha-yat!
Look at Benjie's ha-yat!"

Oh, how red and unhappy Benjie was!

But he laughed as hard as anyone when his tormentors flung the hat into the air, and it caught on the high limb of a tree. He hoped that it would hang there forever. When the hour came to march to the meeting-house, it was very fortunate for Benjie that one of his schoolmates was absent that day, but had left his hat hanging on a nail in the school entry. So Benjie wore it, and was completely satisfied.

He went home that evening to tell Grandmother cheerfully that his new hat was entirely out of reach on the limb of a very tall tree. But the next day, while school was keeping, Grandmother and

Hamish came with a long pole and rescued the hat.

What a craning of necks as the children watched them through the windows! And presently, to the delight of every boy in the room, Grandmother opened the door, and said, "Benjamin Barnett, thee will find thy hat hanging in the entry." For a few hours after that it seemed to Benjie that he didn't even *like* his grandmother!

Soon Benjie began to feel that nothing on earth could harm that hat. For instance, it blew off one day in a windy gust of rain. He carried it home hopefully, for it was smeared with the gummy red clay of North Carolina. But Grandmother let it dry, scraped off the dirt and washed and brushed it carefully. It looked just as good as ever.

"Is this my hat, Grandmother, or is it Grandfather's hat?" asked Benjie.

"It is thy hat now," answered Grandmother.

So, after thinking it over carefully, Benjie argued to himself that he had a perfect right to give the hat to Eliphalet, for it seemed that the little colored boy was the only one in all the world, except

Grandmother, of course, who did not laugh at Benjie's hat.

"Dis heah am a sho-nuff gif'," declared Eliphalet, grinning from ear to ear, and holding the hat reverently in his hands. "Dat ol' Mistuh Beavah, he des' as smoove an' slick as evuh he am."

Eliphalet put on the hat, but it would fall down

over his eyes, and even over his nose. Benjie could see nothing of his friend's face but a pair of grinning lips, a row of white teeth, and a little black chin. Eliphalet had to perch the hat on the back of his head, to be able to see at all. When Benjie went home, feeling generous, but a little doubtful, he looked back and saw Eliphalet strutting all around the cabin as proudly as a king.

But when Dilcey saw the hat decorating her

son's woolly head, she shouted, "Yo-all march
straight up to de big house wid dat hat, an' don' be
delayin' yo'se'f. Benjie's gran'mammy—she gwine
be in a big huff when she fin' dat boy gib ol' dead
Massa's hat away. N' ol' Massa's gwine steal back
an' ha'nt folkses dat weah his hat when dey ain' got
no right."

In a very few moments the hat was lying on
Grandmother's doorstep, and Eliphalet running
home again with all his might and main, for fear of
the *ha'nt.* So the hat was Benjie's once more, and
there was nothing to do but wear it.

Whenever he went to Meeting, he could think
of nothing but his hat. His ears burned scarlet with
shame. He would turn suspiciously, to catch a frosty
twinkle in a pair of elderly eyes, or a smothered
giggle from some boy.

Therefore one morning, as he and Grandmother rode to Meeting, Benjie said, "I guess *thee*
wouldn't wear this hat!"

"Indeed I would, and proud to," answered

Grandmother tartly. And to Benjie's horror, she removed her bonnet and put on the hat, sitting as straight as a ramrod, glancing neither to the right nor the left. She looked ridiculous. Oh, dear! Grandmother was certainly very difficult to look after. He couldn't allow *her* to make a laughing-stock out of herself. Personal pride was one thing, but family pride was another. He sighed. "Never mind, Grandmother. *I'd* better wear it," he said.

Just then a dog came running out from no-where, barking furiously. The horse jumped, and thundered down the road, almost shaking Grand-mother and Benjie to pieces. Afterward it was dis-covered that Benjie's hat was missing. He went back to search for it, praying that it had been trampled beyond repair, or that the dog had carried it off. But no! There it was, lying in a fence corner, with only one small dent in the brim.

"A little steaming and pressing will attend to that," said Grandmother.

"Grandfather certainly bought a good hat,

didn't he?" remarked Benjie.

"Yes," answered Grandmother. "He had the hat made at Beard's Hatter Shop. A good nap beaver will last a lifetime."

Benjie's heart sank. A lifetime seemed a very long time.

So when next Peter Kersey had an errand to Randolph County, Benjie gave him a letter, secretly, with the request that it be delivered to his mother. It said:

Dear Mother—

"I am middling well, and hope thee is the same. Grandmother is well. Jerushy is still alive and shows no sines of dyeing. But I wish thee would send me a Cap, and oblige

Thy obeedyunt son,

Benjie Barnett."

But when Peter returned, and Benjie unwrapped the eagerly-awaited parcel, there was nothing but a yarn muffler. To tie his head up like a baby! Oh, it was terribly disappointing!

CHAPTER V

One evening Benjie sat on a stump in the woods. There was a dark scowl on his face. His lower lip stuck away out. At school that afternoon when Susan Bond was supposed to be doing a sum on the blackboard she had drawn a picture. First she had made a very tall hat. Beneath that, two enormous ears. Then she had drawn a teeny-tiny body, and underneath she had printed BENJIE. She had rubbed it out quickly before the teacher had suspected, but most of the scholars had seen it.

So Benjie, very angry, sat alone on the stump. He was angry at everybody in the world.

Presently Peter Kersey came riding through the wood. He jumped off his horse and sat down by the boy. But Benjie did not speak. He only scowled the darker. Peter picked the hat up and turned it thoughtfully in his hands. "Thy grandfather was a fine man, Benjie," he began quietly, "one of the finest North Carolina has ever produced. He and I were boys together. He was my great friend. Did thee ever hear about the time thy grandfather—" And Peter began telling stories about Grandfather Cox—things that Benjie had never heard before. Soon the scowl faded. The sulky lower lip slipped back. Benjie was smiling, and his eyes were shining. He began to think that perhaps he might wear cheerfully a hat that such a fine grandfather had worn.

"And I'll tell thee, Benjie," said Peter, when he had finished, "Thy grandmother is a fine woman, too. There's no one quite like her. But between me and thee, women never understand just how a man feels about his hat. A man's hat is his own. Let it be suitable, and he can face the world with his head up."

Even if Peter Kersey was an Elder, and sat at the head of the Meeting, he understood a fellow!

But the next morning Benjie remembered Susan's drawing, and he said to himself, "I'll not wear this hat to school if I catch the quinsy and die!" So he took to hiding the hat in the woods, and nobody knew.

One afternoon in the early winter Peter Kersey, with his gun over his shoulder, went into the woods after rabbits. He had bagged three and was just turning homeward, when he saw another plump cotton-tail bounding ahead. He took aim, and missed. The rabbit disappeared into one end of a hollow log just as Peter fired his second shot. He walked forward and peered into the log. And there, in the end of it, was Benjie's hat, with the top of the crown almost torn off by the force of the shot, and the dead rabbit trapped inside!

"Now what have I done?" asked Peter of himself. "I'll have to wait for Benjie to come along this way from school."

When Benjie saw the hat—oh, what joy! "Now I'll never have to wear it again!" he cried.

"Don't thee be too sure of that," warned Peter.

"Thy grandmother is a very resourceful woman. But now we must go and tell her what has happened."

Very slowly Peter and Benjie walked through the woods toward Grandmother's house. Benjie was wondering just how he would explain the fact that his hat was in the end of the log. And Peter was wondering just how he could help Benjie. Presently he said, "A thought has suddenly occurred to me. Put on the hat, boy. And can't thee look a trifle pale?"

Indeed Benjie's cheeks were not so rosy as usual, for what would Grandmother say? What would she do?

Arrived at the house, Peter confronted Grandmother bravely. He kept Benjie well behind him. His face was long and serious.

"I have something to tell thee, Judith," he said. "I hope thee will not take it too hard. This afternoon I was hunting in the woods. And I—I shot thy—thy grandson's hat." He reached around quickly and plucked the hat off Benjie's head.

Grandmother stared at the bullet holes. She saw the stains in the crown. She went white as a sheet. "O Benjie-boy!" she cried. "Is thee hurt?"

Benjie could not bear to see his grandmother looking so white and distressed. But neither could he keep his face straight a moment longer. Laughing, he flung his arms around Grandmother's waist. And then Peter began laughing. And as soon as Grandmother heard about the rabbit, her relief was so great that she laughed as heartily as anyone.

"I do declare," she said, "this hat has had so many misfortunes that I'm beginning to believe the Lord never intended that Benjie should wear it."

"Then thee'll throw it away?" cried Benjie.

"Throw this good hat away?" echoed Grandmother. "Just hearken to him, Peter. I'm sure I don't know where he gets such notions. 'Wilful waste, woeful want,' Grandson. Thee knows that other old saying, too—'Keep a thing seven years, and thee will find a use for it.' So of course I won't throw the hat away. It will come in handy for something one of these days. But thee can't wear it any more. As a matter of fact, Peter," she said, gravely, turning to Peter Kersey, "I don't believe Benjie ever liked this hat, fine as it was. I thought it was very suitable for him. But there's no accounting for a boy's taste. So to-morrow, Benjie, we shall drive over to Friendship and buy thee just an ordinary cap."

An ordinary cap! Why, that was just what Benjie wanted! A fellow didn't have to be careful of an ordinary cap. It was all that Benjie could do to keep from turning a handspring or shouting or clapping his hands. But because of Grandmother's feelings about Grandfather's fine hat, it would never do to shout his joy.

But he ran to the stone jar, and he selected the very biggest and brownest cooky for his friend, Peter Kersey. And the next biggest for himself. As Peter accepted the cooky, he and Benjie looked at each other, as man to man, and smiled.

CHAPTER VI

So Grandmother and Benjie drove over to the general store in Friendship to buy a cap.

Benjie loved to go to the general store. There were so many different kinds of merchandise in it that one could never see them all, unless it could be managed for a boy to stay all day sometime. Benjie wished that he could do that. He would explore and explore. Everything in the general store was in one big dark room. You had to peer closely into corners and behind barrels and boxes to see what was there. But Cyrus Hill, the store-keeper, could go at once and get the very thing you asked for, whether it was flour or coffee or harness or bolts of cloth or nails or iron pots or stick candy or pails or even plows. One could scarcely think of anything that was not tor sale or trade in the general store. It smelled of spice and molasses and cloth and

pickles and cheese and old timber—a perfectly en-
trancing smell.

"Friend Cyrus," said Grandmother, "I wish to
get a cap for my grandson, Benjamin Bartholomew
Barnett. Thee knows, perhaps, that he is spending
the winter with me." Grandmother looked down at
Benjie, and then at Cyrus Hill, as if to say, "There,
Cyrus! Did thee ever see such a fine, upstanding
grandson as mine?"

But of course she would never have dreamed
of doing such boasting aloud.

"Does thee wish to buy or trade, Friend Judith
Cox?" asked Cyrus.

"Tut, tut, Cyrus!" exclaimed Grandmother.
"Does thee think I have much silver? Then thee is
mistaken. But I have for trade four pounds of dried
apples, one dozen eggs, and a pair of socks knit from
the finest yarn. But I doubt if thy caps are worth so
much," added Grandmother.

"I have good caps," said Cyrus. He walked to
the rear of the store, and fished about among some

boxes. Presently he returned with four caps.

Grandmother examined them with the greatest care.

"This one is shoddy, Cyrus," she announced. "It is not worth even one pound of my good dried apples," and Grandmother laid the poor cap down so gently and smiled at Cyrus so kindly that her words bore not the least sting.

"Stand still, Benjie. Thee cannot be looking at everything and try on caps at the same time. Pshaw! That one is too gay. Those checks would fairly shout in Meeting." Grandmother threw a twinkling glance at the store-keeper.

"There now!" exclaimed Cyrus, as Grandmother clapped the third cap on Benjie's head. "That one is very becoming to the boy."

"But this one is better," decided Grandmother, trying the fourth and last cap.

"Doesn't thee think it is a trifle large?" suggested Cyrus.

"All the better," said Grandmother. "Boys

grow, Friend Cyrus, and this cap will last my grandson the longer for being a bit over-size."

So the cap was decided upon, and now Benjie

was free to wander about the store, while Grandmother and the store-keeper politely argued a settlement. Benjie could hear them going on at a great
rate, but little did he care, now that he had his
precious cap upon his head.

But when Benjie and Grandmother climbed
into their carriage once more, Grandmother had
bartered the dried apples and the eggs and the socks
not only for Benjie's cap, but she had a gallon of
molasses as well. And as they left, Cyrus handed
Benjie a stick of hoarhound candy. "Just to show
that I bear thee no ill-will, Judith Cox," said Cyrus.

"Close bargaining is a virtue, Cyrus. Thee
knows that. But thee is a good and honest man. The
next time I come I shall bring thee a batch of my
molasses cookies," promised Grandmother.

Benjie found a cap a great relief after wearing
Grandfather's ponderous hat. On crisp mornings
it could be pulled down over his ears. When he
played at rough games with the other boys it was
never in the way. It could even be jerked off, rolled

up and stuffed into his pocket. It could be worn at
a jaunty angle when he was feeling jaunty himself.
Somehow it matched a fellow's whistling. And when
he was feeling extra skittish, it could be flung high
into the air and caught dexterously as it fell. There
was no doubt that a cap was the right kind of head-
gear for a boy to wear to school.

But when First Day came and Benjie was ready
for meeting, Grandmother studied him doubtfully.
"Thy cap scarcely seems suitable, Benjie," she said.
She removed it from its perch on the back of Benjie's head and set it over his eyes. "Thee ought to
have a good, sober hat to wear to Meeting. 'Tis a
great pity that the nice hat I fixed for thee was
ruined. I trust that folks will not look askance at
the grandson of Judith Cox when they see him wearing an ordinary cap to Meeting."

"Oh, this cap is all right," assured Benjie, as
he rode off with Grandmother. *Today* no one would
smile at seeing him in a strange tall beaver. They
would see just an ordinary boy in an ordinary cap.

And when Benjie took his seat in the meeting-house, he felt as a Friend *should* feel in Meeting—very tranquil and calm, and thankful for all his blessings.

But Benjie had not been sitting there very long before he noticed something unusual about the appearance of Nathan Bond, who sat just in front of him. Nathan was one of Benjie's older schoolmates. He was the miller's son and a brother to Susan, whom Benjie did not like very well, since the day she had drawn his picture on the blackboard. Nathan was a good fellow, though, and today he looked as slick as a whistle in a new hat. Benjie had never seen Nathan look so fine. It was all on account of the hat, because it was undoubtedly a very nice one. It was the kind of a hat that a self-respecting boy ought to have—a round, sensible hat, neither too large, nor too small, but just right. It had been felted of rabbit fur, very carefully, by a skilful hatter. A downy nap of fur had been left on the felt, and it caught the light, as velvet does, whenever Nathan turned his head. Certainly a man would be able to "face the world with his head up," as Peter Kersey had once said, with such a hat as Nathan's. "I wish—" thought Benjie, but then he stopped, for he suddenly remembered that one should not be thinking of worldly things in Meeting.

But afterward, in the meeting-house yard, Benjie talked to Nathan.

"Thee has a fine new hat, Nathan," he said. "Where did thee get it?"

"I trapped twenty rabbits in my box traps," answered Nathan, proudly. "Father took the skins to the hatter and had this hat made from the fur. He paid the hatter twenty-two pounds of flour, too. It's a good hat. I can only wear it for best."

"Of course," agreed Benjie.

On the way home, Benjie made up his mind that he would ask Grandmother if she would allow him to make some box traps. Hamish could help him, or at least show him how to make them. Then he could trap some rabbits and take the skins to a hatter, and have a hat made. But just as he was about to broach the subject to Grandmother, he thought better of it. Perhaps it was really more wise to keep away from the subject of hats for a while. Later, perhaps, Grandmother would remember less vividly the day the horse chewed up his straw hat, and how careless Benjie had been of Grandfather's tall beaver.

Chapter VII

One Seventh Day afternoon Eliphalet and Benjie were playing together. "Let's do something new today," suggested Benjie.

"Us could go 'way off," said Eliphalet.

"Where could we go?" asked Benjie.

Eliphalet waved his hand about vaguely. Then his eyes brightened.

"Us could go down de road, an' ovah de hill, an' long an' long. Pas' de big 'baccy bahn on de nex' plantation. Pas' de' baccy fiel' dat ain' hahdly no en' to. An' long an' long, twell us cut t'roo dat dere Jackson fahm. An' yo' knows what dere, don' yo', Benjie?"

"Thee means the North Carolina Central Railroad track?" asked Benjie.

"Sho'," answered Eliphalet. "Us could go

down dere an' see de big freight go by. Whee-ee-ee! go de big fas' train!"

"All right, let's!" cried Benjie. "Come on!"

So Benjie and Eliphalet set out for the Jackson farm. The railroad ran through one end of it. It was three miles away from Grandmother's farm, but the chance of seeing the train would be worth the trip. Besides, Benjie and Eliphalet were country boys, and accustomed to walking.

It was a crisp winter afternoon, and the feet of the boys were as light as their hearts. It was fun really to be going somewhere, to see something truly exciting, and Benjie thought Eliphalet was pretty smart to think of such an expedition. From Grandmother's farm they could often hear the long whistle of the freight as it sped through the Jackson farm. "Whoooooo! Whoooooo! Who-whooooooooooooo!" it said. But only rarely had they seen the train. The tracks had been laid only the year before.

So they trudged along, talking together, and seeing how far they could kick the same pebble along the road. At last they came to the Jackson farm. They climbed a fence, and cut across some fields, and there was the railroad track, running across the open meadows, the long shining rails disappearing into the distance.

"How soon does thee s'pose the train will come?" asked Benjie.

"Don' zackly know," answered Eliphalet. "But ah knows one come 'long in de aftahnoons somtam. Us ain' missed hit. Ah knows dat. 'Cause dey ain' been no *who-whoo-in*."

After nearly an hour of patient waiting, Benjie cried, "Look, Eliphalet! There it comes! Away off there! See how tiny it looks!"

The boys jumped up and down in their excitement at seeing the train at last.

"Gittin' biggah an' biggah!" cried Eliphalet. "Talkin' loudah an' loudah!"

Now the train was whistling for the crossing. "Whoooooo! Whoooooo! Who-whoooooooooooo!" it said.

Presently they could hear the grind of the wheels. They could hear the puff of the engine. The locomotive loomed up gigantic and black and thunderous. Here it was, rolling past! The engineer leaned from his cab and waved. Now the caboose, followed by car after car, rumbling, grinding, groaning, squeaking. Oh, what a marvelous grand noise the freight train made! The boys stared with big eyes, standing as close to the tracks as they dared.

There! the last car was rumbling by. The instant it had passed the boys jumped on the tracks. In a frenzy of excitement Eliphalet flung his arm in a wide circle, cap in hand. "Whee-eeeeee!" he screamed, sniffing smoke and cinders.

And Benjie, equally excited, jerked off his cap and flung it after that last car. "Wheee-eeeeee!" he screamed.

But suddenly Benjie was tearing down the track after the freight. He was running with all might and main. Because his cap had dropped, as neatly as could be, upon the draw-bar of the last car!

For in Benjie's day the caboose was coupled to the engine, and was not at the rear end of the train, as it is now.

Off sped the train, carrying Benjie's cap, and off sped Benjie, running after it. His feet scarcely touched the earth. His cheeks were red. His breath came hard and panting. His gaze was glued to that cap of his, resting so lightly, but firmly on the draw-bar. But run as hard as he could, Benjie could not run as fast as the train. Away it went, and away went his cap. Off to Durham perhaps, off to Ral-eigh, off to Elizabeth City, off to parts unknown! Benjie's cap had vanished forever from his sight!

He stalked back to where Eliphalet stood, open-mouthed.

"Thee is an *abomination*, Eliphalet!" he cried, angrily.

"Who-all 'bom'nation?" squeaked Eliphalet.

"*Thee* is," declared Benjie. "If thee hadn't brought me over here it would never have happened. And if thee hadn't jerked off thy cap neither would I have. Thee just puts things in my head. That's what thee does!"

Eliphalet had nothing to say, and it was a pair of sad and quiet boys who walked homeward the three long miles. It was dark when they reached the edge of Grandmother's farm. Benjie's steps grew more and more slow. What would Grandmother say this time? Oh, dear! Whoever heard of so many things happening to a fellow's head-gear? First, the straw hat chewed up by a horse. Second, the nap beaver that had been Grandfather's hid in a log and shot to pieces. Third, an ordinary cap carried off no-telling-where by a train.

"Why do people wear hats, anyway?" muttered Benjie.

Eliphalet did not answer. He was feeling very sulky because Benjie had called him a name he had never heard before, but which must mean something dreadful.

But at parting Benjie said, "Well, I guess thee isn't an abomination, after all. I guess I ought to have had more sense than to throw my cap at the train."

"Nossuh! Ah ain' no 'bom'nation," denied Eliphalet, grinning lovingly at Benjie. "Needah is yo' 'bom'nation. *Nobody* ain' no 'bom'nation."

Slowly Benjie found his way in the darkness to Grandmother's house, and saw her plump figure outlined against the window. She was peering out, looking for him.

"Why, Benjie!" she cried, when he entered the door, "I was getting right uneasy about thee. I hadn't seen thee all afternoon. I didn't know where thee had gone. No doubt thee is cold and hungry. I've a good supper for thee. Rachel Kersey brought over a mess of sausage. They've just butchered. And there's gravy and hot cornbread and honey and quince preserves and sweet potato pie. Everything thee likes. So wash thy face and hands while I dish up." Grandmother turned and looked at Benjie more closely. "Grandson," she said, "thee must not run about in cold weather without something on thy head. Thee will take cold."

Grandmother paused, ladle in hand, while she studied Benjie. There had been a very queer, tell-tale expression on his face.

"Benjamin Barnett," she exclaimed, "has something happened to thy cap? No, no, don't thee tell me! Seems as if I couldn't bear it! This is too good a supper to spoil with any tales of disaster. Thee shall tell me later."

So Benjie and Grandmother sat down to the good supper, though Benjie did not care for a second helping of anything, not even of sweet potato pie.

Afterward Grandmother sat back and folded her hands across her apron. She looked at Benjie. "Now, Benjamin, has thee truly lost thy cap? And where? And how?"

But just then came the sound of a terrific squawking. Benjie jumped to his feet, upsetting his chair. He tore out of the house, snatching up a lighted lantern that Hamish had left on the back step after doing the milking. He rushed to the hen-house, and arrived just in time to scare away an opossum. He could see it ambling awkwardly away through the shadows.

"Are the hens all there, Benjie?" called Grand-mother.

Benjie held up the lantern, counting the hens. "Every one of them, Grandmother," he answered.

"Jerushy, too?"

"Yes, Jerushy's safe and sound," shouted Benjie.

When he returned to the house, Grandmother said, "Hamish will have to go 'possum hunting. Only today he was saying how he would relish a roast 'possum in a circle of hot roasted yams." Grandmother smiled. Then she looked down at Benjie. "It was quick-witted of thee to run so fast to the hen-house when thee heard all the commotion. I declare, Benjie, I do not understand thee. Thee is a regular little manbody except as concerns thy head-gear. Now why is that, does thee suppose?"

Benjie confessed that this was a problem beyond him also, and proceeded to tell Grandmother all about his cap, and how it was probably as far as Elizabeth City by this time, and that was a long way off.

"It's a right good thing thy hair is fastened to thy head," stated Grandmother, drily. She got out her knitting needles and a skein of yarn. "I shall knit thee a stocking cap to wear to school. Until I finish it thee will have to tie up thy head in the yarn muffler thy mother sent thee. About a hat to wear to Meeting, that will require some serious thought. I do not know just what can be done about a boy who throws hats away to right and left." Grand-mother shook her head sadly. "Wilful waste, woe-ful want," she said.

The next day was First Day, and Benjie had nothing suitable to wear to Meeting. "Thee cannot go, Benjamin," announced Grandmother. "And since thee cannot go, I shall not go either."

Oh, how dreadful Benjie felt to be the cause of keeping Grandmother away from Meeting! She had not missed a single Meeting for seven years, she said.

But she and Benjie held silent Meeting in Grandmother's best room. Grandmother sat on a straight chair against the wall. She held her hand over her eyes, as she often did at the Meeting-house. She never stirred. And Benjie sat on a straight chair, with his legs dangling, and tried not to wiggle. He had plenty to think about, goodness knows!

At last, after a very long time, Grandmother got up. She crossed the room and shook hands with

Benjie gravely, in the same way that Peter Kersey broke Meeting at the meeting-house by shaking hands with the person who sat next to him in the gallery. The silent meeting held by Grandmother and Benjie was over.

While Grandmother was setting out the cold noon dinner, Peter Kersey came knocking at the door.

"I feared thee was ill, Judith. I did not see thee at Meeting today."

So Grandmother told Peter why she and Benjie had stayed away from Meeting. Benjie felt very small and ashamed while she was talking.

"Now tell me, Friend Peter," said Grandmother, "what can be done with a boy to teach him the value of a hat?"

"What does thee think thyself, Benjie?" asked Peter, kindly. "Does thee have any suggestions at all?"

"I think," said Benjie, slowly, "if I had me some box traps, I could trap me some rabbits. And if I could take the skins to a hatter shop, and have me a good hat made, one made 'spesh'ly for me, I would treat it very careful. A nice hat," said Benjie, dreamily, "neither too large nor too small. A hat like Nathan Bond's."

"Thee is too young to be tinkering with traps," said Grandmother. "And what if I got thee such an expensive hat as that, and some great disaster overtook it, as has happened to thy other hats?

"But there, Peter, we do wrong to discuss such worldly matters on First Day! Will thee be thinking how we can impress my grandson with the proper notions of caring for his things? Thee can help me, Peter. I am greatly concerned. And please to come over soon and we'll talk it over."

So Peter Kersey left, promising Grandmother that he would give this matter of Benjie's careless-ness some serious thought, and that he would return within a day or two.

As Benjie lay in bed that night, he thought to himself, "If I could have a hat as nice as Nathan Bond's, I would never let anything happen to it. Never to a *best* hat like that! A boy would be crazy not to take care of a hat made 'spesh'ly for him out of rabbit fur. A boy would certainly be crazy!"

And as he drifted off to sleep, away off through the dark night he heard a train whistle. "Whoooooo! Whoooooo! Who-whoooooooooooooo!" it said.

Chapter VIII

Grandmother's knitting needles flashed busily, fashioning a stocking cap for Benjie. But every morning until the cap was done, Grandmother tied around Benjie's head the yarn muffler that his mother had sent him from Randolph County.

The boys at school liked Benjie, but they were great ones to tease, and when they saw him wearing the muffler tied 'round his head, some of them shouted "Baby!" and some of them cried, "Got a tooth-ache, Benjie?"

But Benjie had been thinking as he walked through the woods, and now he said, calmly, "It isn't every boy's cap gets to travel on the train! I guess *thy* cap never traveled on the train, Nathan Bond. Nor *thine*, William Brooks. Nor *thine*, Jonathan Gilbert."

And as Nathan Bond and William Brooks and Jonathan Gilbert and every other boy in the school yard gathered about Benjie in a close circle of curiosity, he said, "But *my* cap traveled to Durham, maybe, and maybe to Raleigh, and even as far as Elizabeth City, perhaps. Maybe much, much farther! Maybe to the end of the United States! Anyway, so far that it never came back. That's why

I have to wear this muffler 'til I get something else to wear. 'Cause *my* cap went traveling on the train!"

At first the boys were almost speechless, for none of them had ever traveled on a train, much less their caps. Indeed only one or two of them had even traveled on the stagecoach that rattled over the plank road stretching from Fayetteville to Bethania.

But presently they were bombarding Benjie with questions, and when he had told them all about the strange event that had befallen his cap, they were filled with admiration at his recklessness in throwing his cap at the train in the first place, and with awe at the thought of that cap journeying to far, strange places, the like of which they themselves had never seen. Benjie immediately became quite a hero in their eyes, and when the school bell rang, he could not be seen at all, for he was so closely surrounded by bigger and taller bodies and longer and thicker legs. It was strange and refreshing, but to be expected, that the story of the cap was very different to Benjie's schoolmates than it had been to Grandmother.

Thus the wearing of the hated yarn muffler to school was not so bad after all.

In a day or two Peter Kersey came to Grandmother's house. He had been thinking, as she had asked him to think, and he was ready to discuss this matter of making Benjie more careful concerning his head-gear.

Grandmother and Peter and Benjie sat before the fire in the big cheerful kitchen. Said Peter:

"Friend Judith, it appears to me that thy grandson should have a good hat. A hat made especially to fit his own head. A hat he could wear with satisfaction."

"Goody!" cried Benjie. What a fine friend he had in Peter Kersey!

Grandmother looked at Benjie, whose eyes were full of shining love for Peter. She looked at Peter, whose eyes were full of loving kindness for Benjie. She laid her knitting in her lap. She sniffed

a bit.

"Well, Friend Peter," she said, "I had already come to *that* conclusion myself. I think that no one need to suggest to Judith Cox that she provide a decent hat for her grandson. Her *favorite* grandson," she added, looking sternly at Benjie.

"Of course not, Judith," agreed Peter. "Two wise heads may easily come to the same conclusion. And thee is a wise woman. 'Tis universally agreed."

Grandmother smoothed her apron. "But what I want to know from thee, Peter Kersey, is this," she demanded. "When Judith Cox provides the good hat for her grandson, what is going to make him respect and cherish it?"

"I have thought of that, too," assured Peter. "And here is my suggestion. Thee could put Benjie under contract."

"Under contract!" echoed Grandmother, and her eyes began to twinkle and her mouth to curl up at the corners.

"Under contract!" echoed Benjie. "Is it something like being put in jail?"

"Bless my soul, child!" exclaimed Grandmother. She reached over and smoothed Benjie's hair. "Does thee think thy grandmother would ever do such a dreadful thing as to cast thee into jail? Never, never! But I think Peter has probably thought of a very clever scheme to make thee cherish the fine new hat thee is to have."

"Made of rabbit fur?" cried Benjie. "As fine as Nathan Bond's?"

"Finer, if possible," stated Grandmother, and she looked quickly at Peter Kersey, who was an Elder in the Meeting, to see if he had noticed the boastful thing she had said. So she added, "But of course thee would wear thy fine hat with lowliness of spirit, Benjamin. And now thee run and get a plate of cookies for Peter. And fill one of the pewter mugs with cider for his refreshment."

While Benjie ran to get the cookies and cider for Peter, Grandmother and her neighbor talked together in low tones concerning their plans for Benjie. But he was so excited at the promise of a fine new hat that he paid no attention, and did not even try to hear what they were saying. Only when Peter was ready to leave, he asked, "Is the contract ready to put me under now?"

"No, no!" answered Peter. "We shall have it

ready for thee when thy new hat is done. Thee doesn't understand about the contract yet, but thee will. Thee need have no fears about it."

"What is a contract, Grandmother?" asked Benjie, when Peter had gone.

"The kind of a contract Peter and I are talking about will be an agreement between me and thee. It will be written out on paper. Thee shall sign thy name to it, and I shall sign my name to it. It will be a solemn way of recording a promise. Methinks it will make thee value thy new hat."

"What kind of a promise?" asked Benjie.

"Thee shall see, Grandson," answered Grandmother.

The next day Grandmother pulled the rope that rang the farm bell. It hung on a crosspiece at the top of a long pole in the yard near the house. Whenever Grandmother rang the farm bell, it meant that she wanted Hamish to come to the house.

When Hamish came up through the fields to

answer Grandmother's summons, she said, "Hamish, will thee saddle the horse and ride over to Beard's Hatter Shop? I want thee to find out the charges for making a hat for my grandson, Benjie. A *good* hat, Hamish. The best hat that can be made from rabbit fur."

"Yas'm," said Hamish, his eyes shining with pleasure for Benjie.

"And, Hamish, keep thy wits about thee," advised Grandmother.

"Yas'm," agreed Hamish, touching his forelock, and grinning broadly. Hamish and Grandmother understood and respected each other very well.

Hamish was gone a long time, for it was several miles to Beard's Hatter Shop and back again. When he returned he said:

"De hatter say, ef yo-all kin tote to de shop twenty rabbit skins plus whutsumevah coin er trade dat's wuth one dollah beside, den he mek de fine hat. Ef yo-all ain' got no rabbit skins he git 'em some place elts an' he mek de hat foh t'ree dollahs in coin er trade whutsumevah."

"Thee and thy *whatsomevers!*" exclaimed Grandmother. "Three dollars for a boy's hat? Pshaw, I should have gone myself, and done a bit of bargaining with the hatter."

"T'ree dollahs de reg'lar price foh a fine hat foh boy, de hattah mans say," declared Hamish, "no mattah whut de argymunts."

That evening Grandmother said to Benjie, "How would thee like to go with me to the hatter shop tomorrow, to be measured for thy new hat? Thee may come home from school at noon."

"Oh, goody! I'd like that, Grandmother. But where shall we get the rabbit skins?"

"We shall have to let the hatter furnish the skins. Thee needs the hat, and we cannot wait for Hamish to trap the rabbits. And as I said before, I don't want *thee* tinkering with traps. 'Tis a cruel business, anyway. I'd rather the poor little beasts be shot than trapped.

"And I've been thinking, Benjie. I have decided that I shall trade one of my young pigs in part pay‑ment for the hat. They're nearly three months old now, and worth two dollars apiece. Then I'll take some farm produce to make up the balance if the hatter still insists on charging the high price of three dollars. Therefore, as I think thee should work a bit for thy hat, I have decided that thee may catch the pig. Hamish will make a crate for it in the morning."

"Just watch me catch that pig!" boasted Benjie, happily.

Such an easy way to earn a hat!

Chapter IX

Benjie felt very important leaving school at noon the next day. He ran all the way home.

In the barnyard Hamish was hitching the horse to the carriage. On the ground near by was the crate he had made to hold the pig. And on the rear seat of the carriage were some tow bags, filled with turnips that were to help pay for the hat.

"Benjie, get into thy farm clothes," said Grandmother. "I think thee had better catch the pig before dinner. Thee will not be so agile after thee eats. And little pigs are always agile."

So Benjie ran to put on his old farm clothes. And while he was dressing he thought up a riddle. Perhaps not a real riddle, but something like one.

"Grandmother," he shouted, "guess this riddle. When does P-I-G spell H-A-T?"

Grandmother's cheeks crinkled with laughter. She pretended to think a while. "Perhaps I know," she said at last. "P-I-G spells H-A-T when a certain pig becomes a certain hat at the hatter shop."

"Oh, thee is smart, Grandmother," complimented Benjie. "I didn't think thee could guess it so quickly."

Benjie snatched a cooky and ran to the barnyard. He thought it would be great fun to catch the little pig. The sooner he caught it the sooner he would have his hat.

The pigs were rooting about in the low ground that lay south of the big barn. It was nice muddy ground. At least the pigs thought it was nice, for except in very dry weather a pool of water was always there in which they could wallow.

Benjie looked at the pigs. He decided he would catch that chunky little fellow with the black spot on his shoulder and the extra curly tail.

But first he slipped into the barn and gathered up an armful of corn. He would pretend to be feeding the pigs. Then all of a sudden, *pounce*, he would have his pig! It would be easy. "Just watch Benjie Barnett!" he said to himself.

So with careless air, he walked down the slope toward the pigs. He called "Here, piggy-piggy-piggy! Here, piggy-piggy-piggy!"

And while he scattered the ears of corn, and kept an eye on the pig of his choice, the greedy animals crowded about him, grunting and pushing.

All of a sudden Benjie flung down the last ear of corn, and made a grab for the little pig. His hands slid over its smooth hide. "I've got him!" he cried. "No! Yes! Oh, get out of the way, thee great big hog, thee! Quit jostling, while I hold this little fellow! Oh, shucks!" For the pig had slipped out of Benjie's hands as easily as a slab of lard!

Away bounded Chunky Pig! Around the barnyard, up the slope he went, and away went Benjie after him! Around and around the barn they ran. A dozen times Benjie was just in the very act of snatching up the little pig, but every time Chunky slipped out of his hands. Benjie thought that surely there could be nothing on earth so slippery as that little pig.

"I'll play a trick on him!" thought Benjie. And he got Chunky to running around the barn as fast as possible, and then Benjie started around the other way. They met at one corner of the barn, Benjie plunging pell-mell, and the little pig doing a kind of teeter-totter from one end of his sausage-shaped body to the other in slowing up a bit. Benjie and the little pig were both surprised at the sudden meeting.

Benjie stumbled over Chunky and fell flat just as the pig wavered for a moment and then darted between Benjie's legs. Benjie fell right on top of Chunky! How that little pig squealed! How that little pig squirmed!

"Help, Hamish!" cried Benjie, trying to hold the pig. "Help!"

But Hamish was too weak to stir. He was hanging over the barnyard fence as limp as a rag, for he had laughed and laughed and laughed until he could laugh no more at the sight of Benjie chasing the pig. He could only gasp, and groan, and wipe his tears away. And yonder, on the back porch of the house, stood Grandmother, and she, too, was leaning up against a post, spent with laughter.

Now came Eliphalet, his legs twinkling with speed. "What-all gwine on heah?" he cried, just as the little pig slipped out from under Benjie and ran away.

"Shucks!" said Benjie. He stood up and stared, mud-spattered and scowling, at Eliphalet. "I bet thee couldn't catch a pig. I bet thee couldn't *ever* catch a pig! Let's see thee catch one!"

"Ah ain' saying kin ah ketch dat pig er kin ah not ketch um. But effen yoh wants, ah'll holp yo-all," offered Eliphalet.

Poor little Chunky! He was just beginning to breathe more easily when here came that pestiferous boy again. Two of him, in fact!

Such a scattering of all the pigs when Benjie and Eliphalet ran down the slope and right into their midst. How many times the boys fell into the mud no one could count! *Splash,* went the muddy water of the pool when Eliphalet fell into it! What stars the boys saw when they collided and cracked their heads together, their heads that seemed as hard as the hardest rocks! How dizzily they staggered for a moment! How furious they were when the little pig played a trick on them and dashed through the barn door and out through a hole on the other side. It took them several moments to catch up with him again. And oh, how many times

they almost caught Chunky, only to feel him slide
away from them!

But at last Chunky dashed through the barnyard gate and out into the house-yard. And
whether he lost his bearings in less familiar territory,
or whether he became too tired to run any longer,
there came a glorious moment when Benjie fell
upon him, and managed to hold him until Eliphalet

ran to help, and Hamish came with the crate. They popped him into it, to the tune of his terrific squealing, and the boys' hoarse shouting. Hamish nailed down some laths. Then they all stood off to look at Chunky Pig, who was poking his pink snout between the bars of the crate.

"Whew!" sighed Benjie, wiping a chunk of mud off his forehead.

"Guess yo-all done earn dat hat yo' gwine git!" laughed Hamish.

Benjie thought so, too, and even after he had scrubbed himself clean, and put on his good clothes, and eaten three helpings of everything at dinner, he was still red from the mighty exertions of chasing the slippery little pig.

At last he put on his stocking cap that Grandmother had finished, and they climbed into the carriage, with Chunky and the turnips safely stowed away in the rear. Off to Jamestown they rode, and when they got there, Benjie ran into the general store to ask the storekeeper the market price of turnips.

"Forty cents a bushel today, Grandmother," he announced, climbing back into the carriage.

"Then two-and-one-half bushels will pay the extra dollar for thy hat," said Grandmother.

About a mile north of Jamestown was Beard's Hatter Shop. It had been there for many years. Everybody in the countryside knew of it. David Beard, who had made the establishment famous, was no longer there. The shop was managed for David's widow by Isaac Lilly.

It was a square brick building, with its blank windowless side to the road. East of the shop was the big brick house where the Beard family lived. North of it lay a thick oak woods, out of which spring water flowed down to a tan-yard, for Benjie soon discovered that not only hats were made at the hat shop, but also boots and shoes, saddles and saddle-bags, hair trunks, and many other useful articles of leather. The shelves along one wall of the shop were stocked with all the merchandise that the hatter made and had for sale, as well as the many different kinds of things that his customers had traded in for hats.

When Grandmother told Isaac Lilly that Benjie's grandfather had bought a hat there in 1838, the hatter lifted down a thick old ledger from one of the shelves. He turned its yellowed pages, and there, as plainly as if it had been written yesterday by David Beard the hatter, was the record:

Ninth Month, 12th day, 1838

One nap beaver for Julian Cox @ $8.00

Settlement made by Julian Cox, as follows:

For his old hat	$1.00
For one barrel of cider	$2.00
For painting the gig of my father-in-law	5.00
Total	$8.00

Account closed, Ninth Month, 29th day, 1838.

David Beard

"There, thee sees how thy grandfather paid for *his* hat, Benjie!" said Grandmother, proudly.

"And I'll warrant the hat is still as good as

ever," said Isaac Lilly, smiling.

Grandmother looked down her nose at Benjie, whose cheeks turned as red as the wattles of a turkey-cock.

"But now let us talk of thy making a hat for my grandson," said Grandmother, briskly veering away from such an embarrassing subject. But she was so pleased with Isaac Lilly for showing them the ledger and the record of that old transaction that she fairly purred. For once she did no dickering.

"I know thy hats are good hats," she said. "And if thee has set thy price at three dollars, there is no more to say."

And after Isaac had been out to take a look at the pig, and had agreed to accept the little porker as payment, together with two-and-a-half bushels of turnips, he proceeded to measure Benjie for the hat. Chills of happy excitement coursed down Benjie's spine.

"Now," said Isaac kindly, when the measuring was done, "would thee like to see the process of making the hats? I hear tell that there's some new-fangled machinery now for hat-making. But what was good enough for David Beard is good enough for me, and as long as this shop can turn out good hats by hand, we'll do it."

So Isaac showed his customers how the fur was cut from the pelts with long-handled shears, and how the fur and the hair were separated.

"And now here is my assistant bowing the fur."

There was a pile of fur lying on a bench. It had been slipped under a heavy cord of cat-gut that was fastened to one end of the bench. The cord was drawn taut by a hickory bow fastened to the other end. It was something like the bow of a violin, only five or six times as large. The assistant was snapping this bow with his fingers, so that it snapped against the fur, and beat it into smaller and finer particles.

Then Isaac showed how the sheets of bowed fur were dipped into vats of boiling water, and rolled and dipped again, and how it was coated with shellac and kneaded like dough until it was smooth.

"Now when this is done," said Isaac, "we are ready to cut a piece from the *dough* to make a particular hat. We press this into a thin circular piece, with these special tools here, and allow it to dry. After that it goes into a warm solution again, and while it is wet we heat and press and smooth it until we get the proper thickness and softness. And now here are the wooden blocks or shapes on which we mold the felt. It dries to the shape of the block. When we take it off and add the lining and the band, the hat is finished."

" 'Tis very interesting, Isaac Lilly," said Grandmother. "I'm sure my grandson ought to take good care of his hat since he has seen the vast amount of work that goes into its making. Now when will it be done?"

"My son John will be delivering some other hats in thy neighborhood next Seventh Day," said Isaac. "He will also deliver thy grandson's hat."

"Thank thee for getting a hat made for me, Grandmother," said Benjie on the way home. 'Tis very good of thee."

"I am glad to furnish thee a hat, Benjie, if thee appreciates it and takes care of it," answered Grandmother. "Thee knows that the little pig would some day have provided me with meat for nigh a whole winter. Two-and-a-half bushels of turnips would also have lasted me a long time. So thee understands that thy hat is an expensive hat."

"My!" exclaimed Benjie. "I should say so!"

CHAPTER X

On Seventh Day Benjie could scarcely keep his mind on his morning chores, because every two minutes he was rushing to see if Isaac Lilly's son had arrived with the hat. Grandmother had invited Peter and Rachel Kersey to come to supper that evening, and it seemed to Benjie that everything she gave him to do kept him away from the front of the house and a view of the road. Finally he stationed Eliphalet on the front doorstep as chief look-out, but by noon the little colored boy was weary, and had about given up hope.

"Maybe de hoss run away," he suggested, "an bus' de hat."

Benjie flew to Grandmother. "Eliphalet says maybe the horse ran away," he cried, "and busted the hat."

"Such language!" exclaimed Grandmother. "And calm thyself, Benjamin. 'Tis unseemly of thee to get so wrought up. And shame on thee, Eliphalet, for borrowing trouble. Isaac Lilly promised the hat for today. It will arrive in good time."

Just then there was a clatter of hoofs on the frozen ruts of the lane. Benjie and Eliphalet rushed to the window. There was a young horseman alighting.

"It's the hat, Grandmother!" shrieked Benjie.

"De hat am came, Gran'mammy!" yelled Eliphalet.

"The roof of the house will fly off with all your shouting," laughed Grandmother. "Now mind your manners, both of you, and keep yourselves calm." But Grandmother's own cheeks were flushed with excitement as she hurried to the door.

And when Isaac Lilly's son had gone, munching a thick molasses cooky, Grandmother held Benjie's new hat at arm's length, carefully, while she and the boys gazed at it, spellbound with admiration.

"Isaac Lilly has done a fine piece of work for thee, Benjie," she said.

Benjie could not speak. He reached out a trembling finger to smooth the shining nap of the crown. Eliphalet's little black finger stretched forth timidly, also, to touch Benjie's wonderful hat.

But Grandmother held it beyond their reach. "There now!" she exclaimed, setting it on the high ledge of the mantel. "We shall put it up here for the present, where it can be seen, but not touched. And now thee come to dinner, Benjie. Thee is welcome to stay, Eliphalet, but I know thy mother expects thee at home."

So Eliphalet went home, reluctantly. In less than an hour he was back again, accompanied by Hamish and Dilcey, who had come to see Benjie's hat. They stood in a row before the mantel, with Benjie and Grandmother, gazing at Isaac Lilly's masterpiece. At least Benjie considered it undoubtedly the finest hat that had ever come out of Beard's Hatter Shop.

Presently Hamish touched his forelock, and said, "Miss Judit', ef yoh could 'low Benjie to come to de cabin nex' Choosday evenin', me an' Alec an' Phin, we gwine pick de banjo. We gwine mek de bes' music we knows how to mek. Com'ratin' Benjie's new hat."

Grandmother looked at the three shining smiles of Hamish and Dilcey and Eliphalet, and she looked at Benjie's pleading eyes.

"I do not hold with so much fuss being made over so worldly a thing as a mere hat," she answered, though at this point her admiring glance *would* stray to the mantel. "Neither do I much favor thy heathenish music, Hamish. But I haven't the heart to rebuff thy kindness. So Benjie may come on the evening of Third Day. He may stay one hour."

"We mek much music in one houah, Ma'am," said Hamish. "T'anks foh de priv'lege. Now Dilcey and me we do yo' Sat'day scrubbin' foh yo-alls."

"That will give me plenty of time to wash Benjie's hair for the wearing of the new hat tomorrow," said Grandmother.

After Benjie's hair was washed, he must sit by the fireside, for fear of catching cold, though no one would have been able to coax him out of the house, not with his precious hat within sight at last!

But when Hamish and Dilcey and Eliphalet

had gone home, and the house was clean and quiet and shining, Grandmother said, "I've had no time to gather the eggs today. Come, Benjie. Thy hair is good and dry now. Pull thy stocking cap well over thy ears, and thee may help me gather the eggs."

So Grandmother and Benjie went to the barn to gather the eggs. They went to the hen-house, too.

"Look, Grandmother," whispered Benjie, with a little giggle, "there is Jerushy sitting on a nest. She's just pretending."

"Poor old Jerushy!" smiled Grandmother. "Though she's too old to lay eggs, I suppose she still clings to the habits of her egg-laying days, and sits on a nest every day. She's too ignorant to realize that she'll never lay another one."

But just then Jerushy stood up on her nest. She jerked her head about as if to say, "Is *that* so, Judith Cox?" And then she stepped off the nest, and set up an excited cackling. It was rather a hoarse cackle, and not so very loud, for Jerushy's vocal cords were just as old as Jerushy.

"Cut-cut-cut-cad*aw*ket! Cut-cut-cut-cad*aw*ket!" cackled Jerushy.

"Grandmother!" cried Benjie.

"Benjie! *Jerushy!*" cried Grandmother, and she and Benjie rushed to the nest.

And there lay a tiny round egg!

Grandmother picked it up, still warm. She and Benjie stared at it.

"'Tis a miracle!" whispered Grandmother. Her cheeks were quite pale. Actually there were tears in her eyes! "After all these years!" Grandmother breathed softly. "Our old Jerushy! Nobody ever heard of the like!" And Grandmother laid the egg carefully in the nest again, and she picked up the old speckled hen and stroked her feathers, and crooned over her tenderly.

And as Benjie and Grandmother returned to the house, with Jerushy's tiny egg in the center of the mound of big eggs in the basket, Grandmother said, "This is a great event. Ring the bell for Hamish. I just *must* tell somebody!"

So once more Hamish came up through the fields, and there was much exclaiming over Jerushy's egg.

"Of course it isn't a normal egg," said Grandmother. "It's very small, and probably it has no yelk. But bless Jerushy's old heart!" Tenderly she laid the little egg in the nest of the glass hen on the mantel, and covered it over.

And Benjie, seeing it there close to his hat, cried, "Grandmother! Maybe Jerushy laid the egg because of my new hat!"

Grandmother smiled. "Today thee thinks that everything has to do with thy hat."

"Com'ratin' Benjie's hat," chuckled Hamish, as he went off home again. But he hadn't gone far before his steps began to lag. He stopped and scratched his head. "Ah plum disremembe'd ah got bizness ovah in town," he muttered. "So ah saddles de hoss and ah goes."

And before evening everyone in the country-side had heard how "Judith Cox's ancient hen," at thirteen years of age, had laid an egg!

" 'Tis one of those freaks of Nature for which there's no accounting," said the neighbors.

But Benjie felt that Jerushy, who was almost like a member of the family, had laid her miraculous egg to celebrate the arrival of his new hat!

CHAPTER XI

In the early dusk came Peter and Rachel Kersey, to take supper with Grandmother and Benjie. And after they had admired Benjie's hat and Jerushy's egg, they sat down to the table.

Grandmother had out her best silver, the thin, hand-made silver that had belonged to her mother. The table was loaded with Grandmother's delicious cooking. At one end there was a roast chicken, brown and sizzling. At the other end there was a round of roast pork. In between there were large dishes of mashed turnips and boiled potatoes and pickles and preserves and jellies and jams. There was a big cake on the table and a plate of cookies. There was a whole pound of butter, with a rose imprinted on the top. There was a platter bearing two sweet potatoes, and if you do not think this was enough for Peter and Rachel and Grandmother and Benjie, then you have never seen any North Carolina sweet potatoes, or yams, as they were called. They were so enormous that the two of them would have been enough to feed Hamish and Clemmie and Eliphalet as well, and plenty to spare.

There was a glass dish holding a comb of honey that looked as if it had been carved from the purest, most delicate amber, for North Carolina is a land of honey, too. When Benjie broke off a helping for himself with the big silver spoon, the carving crushed delicately into a syrup so thick that it would scarcely spread on his buttered biscuit. To wind up the feast there was persimmon pudding with cream.

And after supper, when they were all gathered around the fire, Peter reached into his pocket and drew out some papers.

"I have the contract for thee, Benjie," he said. Rachel squeezed Benjie's hand reassuringly, and while he watched with round eyes, Grandmother drew up the little cherry table that had a fluted edge like pie-crust. She brought the ink, and the quill pen that had been Grandfather's, and the shaker of fine sand to blot the ink.

Peter put on his spectacles, and peered over them at Benjie. "Thee may come and look over my shoulder, but I shall read the contract aloud, so that thee will be sure to understand it."

So Benjie stood at Peter's shoulder, and Rachel drew her chair close and slipped her arm around Benjie. Grandmother stood back of him, looking down at the papers spread on the table. Peter read the contract. It said:

"I, Benjamin Bartholomew Barnett, have this day received from my grandmother, Judith Cox, one hat made of rabbit fur, for which she paid in trade to the firm of Beard's Hatter Shop a sum amounting to three dollars.

I hereby promise and agree for reasons understood by me and my grandmother, Judith Cox, that when I reach man's estate, I will repay unto said Judith Cox the sum of three dollars, this sum either to be in silver coin, or in the form of one three-month-old pig and two-and-one-half bushels of turnips, in which form of trade said Judith Cox paid for said hat of rabbit fur.

In witness whereof I have hereunto set my hand and seal this 7th day of Second Month, in the year of our Lord, 1857."

When Peter had finished reading the contract, he handed the pen to Benjie and said, "Now, if thee agrees, thee is to sign thy name."

So Benjie, with his tongue between his teeth, signed the contract in his best hand-writing. And Grandmother signed, and Peter and Rachel Kersey signed their names as witnesses.

"When shall I reach man's estate?" asked Benjie.

" 'Twill be when thee is twenty-one years of age, Grandson, and that is a long way off," answered Grandmother. She smoothed Benjie's hair, and for some reason her eyes were moist. She looked reproachfully at Peter Kersey.

"'Tis over-solemn, Peter," she said, "and I have my doubts that I like this contract, after all."

"Now, now, Judith," answered Peter, smiling,

and shaking sand over the signatures. "Thee well knows this is a mere form. 'Twould never stand legally, for Benjie is too young to be making any legal agreements.

"Now, Benjie," he added, turning to the boy at his shoulder, "I shall explain to thee that this is a mere device to make thee value thy hat. But I would impress upon thee that thy word is as good as thy bond, and a promise is a promise. I think thee will repay thy grandmother the price of thy hat, and enjoy doing it, when thee reaches man's estate."

Benjie nodded vigorously. He turned and hugged his grandmother around the waist. "Of course I'll pay her back," he cried. "I bet I'll pay her *two* pigs and *three* bushels of turnips!"

"Bless thee, Grandson, but don't thee be too rash," said Grandmother, smiling down at Benjie, as were Peter and Rachel.

"Thee is a good boy, Benjie," said Peter, "in spite of all thy troubles with thy various hats. I doubt not thee will grow up to be a good man some day—a man who will be careful of what he owns."

"A man who will say to his own children, 'Wilful waste, woeful want'," added Grandmother.

So Peter and Rachel went home, and Grandmother tucked the contracts into the big Bible for safe keeping, one copy for Benjie, and one for herself.

CHAPTER XII

The next day was First Day. Benjie was ready for Meeting long before the hour. At last Grandmother lifted down the hat from the mantel. She set it carefully on Benjie's head. She tipped up his chin and looked at him.

"Thee is a fine little manbody," she said, "and thee looks as the grandson of Judith Cox ought to look when he goes to Meeting."

While Grandmother was putting on her bonnet, Benjie scrambled up on a chair, that he might see himself in the little oval mirror that hung in Grandmother's bedroom. Ah, there he was, a round and shining face under a round and shining hat! A hat that was neither too large nor too small, but just right!

"Tut, tut!" cried Grandmother, when she saw

him gazing, charmed, into the mirror. "Thy hat
must not make thee vain. Remember 'tis a mere

decency, and not an ornament to gloat upon."

When they parted at the meeting-house door, she said as usual, "Now thee be a good boy, Grandson," and she added, "Let not thy hat tempt thee to worldly thoughts."

And as Benjie sat all by himself on the men's side of the meeting-house, he remembered Grandmother's words. But he said to himself, "In a little while, when I have grown sort of used to it, I'll stop thinking about my new hat."

But it was no more than human first to enjoy thinking how very well the hat looked on him, and how very respectable it made him feel.

How could he help wishing that Milo and Matthew could gaze upon him at this moment? And his mother and father, too. And Hannah, and Narcissa Clementina, though it was doubtful if that least one were old enough to appreciate a brother's fine appearance.

And would not any boy want to think with joy of the coming of Third Day evening, when Alec and

Phin would come knocking on Grandmother's door, with their banjos under their arms? Benjie would ride pick-a-back on Alec's strong shoulders. They would go loping across the fields to Hamish's cabin, which would be filled with dancing fire-light and music and laughter—all for Benjie!

And there was Jerushy, the dear old speckled hen. Could one forget her generosity in helping to celebrate the new hat with her miraculous egg?

But the crowning thought of all was the memory of the contract, tucked away in Grandmother's Bible. How grown-up and responsible that made him feel! Just like a man would he some day settle a man's honest debts! Indeed he would take excellent care of this very suitable hat that made a fellow "able to face the world with his head up"—this hat that he was to pay for when he reached "man's estate"—this hat that was to help him grow into a man careful and steady and wise like his father, like his grandfather, like his friend Peter Kersey.

Benjie looked at Peter, there in the gallery facing the Meeting. And to his great surprise, he saw Peter reach over and shake hands with the person next to him. Why, Meeting was over! Whoever would have thought that the moments could have passed so quickly?

Alas! Benjie had spent the whole time thinking about his hat!

"What would Grandmother say if she knew?" thought Benjie to himself. "But 'tis the first day I've worn my new hat. After this I shall sit in Meeting and not think about it at all." And as the people moved out of the meeting-house, Benjie sent a swift little prayer Heavenward, asking forgiveness.

In the meeting-house grounds, Nathan Bond said, "Thee has a fine new hat, Benjie."

"It's my *best* hat, Nathan," answered Benjie.

"Of course," agreed Nathan.

And all the boys and girls gathered 'round, to admire Benjie's wonderful new hat!

THE END.

Date Due

My 30 5	APR 14 '70	NOV 26 '85	
Je 26 5?	MAY 13 '70	MAY 7 '90	
De 8 5?	APR 21 '7?		
My 22 53	MAY 14 '71		
No 29 5?	MAR 27 '73		
De 12 55	APR 13 '73		
Ja 19	APR 8 '75		
Mr 7 56			
Mr 29 56			
Mr 1 57			
Ja 31 58			
NOV 3 '60	OCT 20 '78		
DEC 14 '6?	MAR 9 '78		
MAR 12 '65	NOV 11 '85		
Wynnesburg	OCT. 14 1988		
DEC 17 '69			
MAR 11 '70			
MAR 31 '70			